T
J

JIGSAW
JONES
MYSTERY

YUBA COUNTY LIBRARY
MARYSVILLE

# The Case of the Kidnapped Candy

by James Preller
illustrated by Jamie Smith
cover illustration by R. W. Alley

A
LITTLE APPLE
PAPERBACK

SCHOLASTIC INC.
New York Toronto London Auckland Sydney
Mexico City New Delhi Hong Kong Buenos Aires

*For Maria Barbo, who knows Jigsaw better than he knows himself.*

If you purchased this book without a cover, you should be aware that this book is stolen property. It was reported as "unsold and destroyed" to the publisher, and neither the author nor the publisher has received any payment for this "stripped book."

No part of this work may be reproduced, stored in a retrieval system, or transmitted in any form or by any means, electronic, mechanical, photocopying, recording, or otherwise, without written permission of the publisher. For information regarding permission, write to Scholastic Inc., Attention: Permissions Department, 557 Broadway, New York, NY 10012.

ISBN-13: 978-0-439-89618-4
ISBN-10: 0-439-89618-5

Text copyright © 2007 by James Preller.
Illustrations copyright © 2007 by Scholastic Inc.

All rights reserved. Published by Scholastic Inc.

SCHOLASTIC, LITTLE APPLE, JIGSAW JONES, and associated logos are trademarks and/or registered trademarks of Scholastic Inc.

12 11 10 9 8 7 6 5 4 3 2 1 7 8 9 10 11 12/0

Special thanks to Robin Wasserman

Printed in the U.S.A.
First printing, January 2007

YUBA COUNTY LIBRARY
MARYSVILLE

# Read all the Jigsaw Jones Mysteries!

- ☐ #1 The Case of Hermie the Missing Hamster
- ☐ #2 The Case of the Christmas Snowman
- ☐ #3 The Case of the Secret Valentine
- ☐ #4 The Case of the Spooky Sleepover
- ☐ #5 The Case of the Stolen Baseball Cards
- ☐ #6 The Case of the Mummy Mystery
- ☐ #7 The Case of the Runaway Dog
- ☐ #8 The Case of the Great Sled Race
- ☐ #9 The Case of the Stinky Science Project
- ☐ #10 The Case of the Ghostwriter
- ☐ #11 The Case of the Marshmallow Monster
- ☐ #12 The Case of the Class Clown
- ☐ #13 The Case of the Detective in Disguise
- ☐ #14 The Case of the Bicycle Bandit
- ☐ #15 The Case of the Haunted Scarecrow
- ☐ #16 The Case of the Sneaker Sneak
- ☐ #17 The Case of the Disappearing Dinosaur
- ☐ #18 The Case of the Bear Scare
- ☐ #19 The Case of the Golden Key

☐ #20 The Case of the Race Against Time

☐ #21 The Case of the Rainy-Day Mystery

☐ #22 The Case of the Best Pet Ever

☐ #23 The Case of the Perfect Prank

☐ #24 The Case of the Glow-in-the-Dark Ghost

☐ #25 The Case of the Vanishing Painting

☐ #26 The Case of the Double-Trouble Detectives

☐ #27 The Case of the Frog-jumping Contest

☐ #28 The Case of the Food Fight

☐ #29 The Case of the Snowboarding Superstar

And Don't Miss . . .

☐ Jigsaw Jones' SUPER SPECIAL #1: The Case of the Buried Treasure

☐ Jigsaw Jones' SUPER SPECIAL #2: The Case of the Million-Dollar Mystery

☐ Jigsaw Jones' SUPER SPECIAL #3: The Case of the Missing Falcon

☐ Jigsaw Jones' SUPER SPECIAL #4: The Case of the Santa Claus Mystery

☐ Jigsaw Jones' Detective Tips

# Contents

# Chapter One
## The L Word

Love stinks.

Don't get me wrong. I like love. I *love* love. I love my mom and dad, jigsaw puzzles, grape juice, and the New York Mets.

Some days, I even love my big brothers.

At least, on days they're not calling me Worm. Or Shorty. Or Peanut.

But, as my mom likes to say, everything has its place. Even love. It belongs in gushy birthday cards from my aunt Harriet. Good-night kisses. Those weird cooing noises

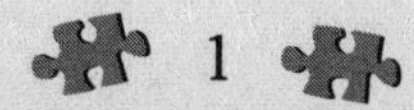

everyone makes when there's a baby around.

Here's where it *doesn't* belong:

On the baseball field.

At the dentist.

In Room 201.

And that's how all the trouble started. Because this week, Room 201 was all about love.

Right after Valentine's Day, our teacher, Ms. Gleason, started us on a new unit: poetry. *Love* poetry.

We read lots of poems. None of them made much sense.

*How do I love thee, let me count the ways.*

*Love looks not with the eyes,*
*but with the mind.*

*Love's not time's fool.*

LOVE
POEM

Give me a break. I mean, who talks like that, anyway? Yeesh.

All those lines were written by this guy William Shakespeare, about four hundred years ago. Ms. Gleason says he was the greatest English writer in history.

*I* say he's not even writing in English. It sounds like gibberish to me.

On Monday morning, after a whole week of that stuff, we all came to class hoping to wave our poetry unit good-bye. The day started with good news.

"We've almost finished our poetry unit," Ms. Gleason said. Lots of the guys cheered. Someone whistled. It could have even been me.

But I should have known better. Good news and bad news are like lightning and thunder. When you see one, you know the other is coming. And I didn't have long to wait.

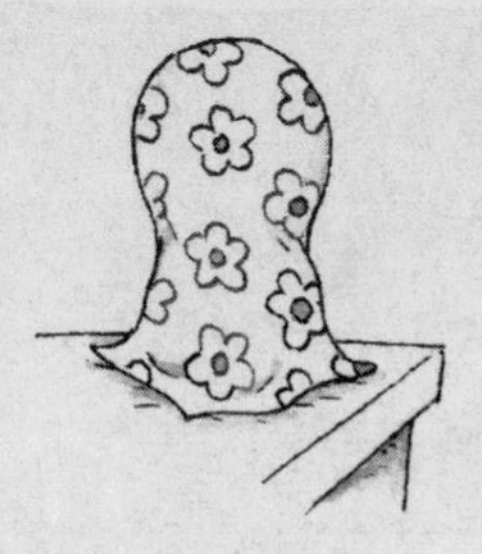

# Chapter Two

## The Bad News

"This week, you will all write your *own* poems about something you love," Ms. Gleason said.

Me? Write a mushy, gushy love poem? Oh, brother.

We helped Ms. Gleason make a list of the things that went into a poem. When we were done, these words were written up on the board:

Rhyme Sounds Rhythm Form
Syllables Words Letters Ideas

"Which one is most important?" asked Athena Lorenzo.

"What do you think, class?" Ms. Gleason asked.

Ralphie Jordan said rhyme.

Kim Lewis said words.

Bigs Maloney pounded his hand on his desk and said it had to be syllables.

Soon we were all shouting out answers. Suddenly we heard Ms. Gleason clap softly, *clap, clap.* We clapped back three times, *CLAP CLAP CLAP.* It was our sign to be quiet.

So we were.

Geetha Nair raised her hand. "Maybe they're all important," she said in a very small, quiet voice. "Maybe they work together."

Ms. Gleason smiled at her. "I think that's exactly right, Geetha. Every piece of a poem has its own job to do. And now *you* all have jobs to do. So take out a blank piece of paper and start brainstorming."

Brainstorming meant we should write down anything that popped into our heads. Later, we would turn it into a nice, neat poem.

I tried to brainstorm. I really did. But all I could come up with was a brain drizzle. We

scritch-scratched away at our poems for ten minutes. Then Ms. Gleason told us to put our papers away.

"You'll have a chance to work on these every morning this week," she said. "On Friday, we will read them out loud and then celebrate with a special surprise."

Lucy Hiller raised her hand. "What is it?"

Ms. Gleason smiled her special, supersecret smile. "If I told you that, it wouldn't be a surprise."

The class groaned. We hated waiting. But we *loved* surprises.

"Can you give us a hint?" Mila Yeh asked. She looked at me and slid her finger across her nose. It was our secret sign. She was my detective partner, after all, and good detectives always have secret signals. I knew exactly what she was thinking. If Ms.

Gleason gave us a hint, maybe Mila and I could solve the puzzle. That's what we do best.

"Two hints," Ms. Gleason agreed. "One, it's under this sheet." She pointed to a bright pink flowered sheet. It was draped over a lumpy object on the corner of her desk. "Here's your second hint. Since you're writing poems about something you love, your special treat will be something *I* love. And I think you're going to love it, too."

Yeesh. There was that word again. What would a teacher love?

Homework?

Chalk?

Pencils?

But Ms. Gleason said we would love it, too. So it couldn't be anything like that . . . right?

This wasn't just a surprise, it was a mystery. And when you're a private detective, there's plenty to love about that.

# Chapter Three

## A Blank Page

Nicole Rodriguez decided to write a limerick about her goldfish, Goldie. Eddie Becker was writing an ode to baseball and Albert Pujols. Mila was working on a poem about spaghetti and meatballs.

And me?

On Tuesday, I decided to write about grape juice. Wednesday, I switched to jigsaw puzzles. Wednesday night, I changed my mind again. And then again on Thursday morning. I was changing my mind more often than a traffic light changes colors.

By Thursday night, I was desperate. The poem was due on Friday. But all I had to show for the week was a blank sheet of paper.

Maybe I could tell Ms. Gleason I had come up with a new kind of poem — the invisible kind.

I knew what the problem was. Every time I started thinking about my poem, I ended up thinking about our surprise. I wanted to know what was under that sheet. I *needed* to know.

It was too big to be a pile of comic books.

It was too small to be a sled.

It was too quiet to be a new class pet.

I was stumped.

Ms. Gleason wasn't handing out any more hints. And she had told us *not* to peek under the sheet. She just kept saying we'd have to wait and see.

Grown-ups love to wait and see.

Don't ask me why.

I flopped down on my bed. My dog, Rags, jumped up next to me. He stuck his cold, wet nose into my hand. Then he wiped his tongue up the side of my face. *Slurp!*

"What should I write about, Rags?" I asked. He didn't know, either. He just wagged his tail and plopped his head down on my chest. That's Rags for you. He's always there when I need him. He's the best friend a guy could have.

That was it!

I hopped out of bed and ran to my desk. I grabbed a pencil. I squinched up my eyes and bent over the blank page.

I wrote and wrote. I crossed things out and scribbled away. An hour later, I was curled up in bed, fast asleep. My poem was tucked away in my backpack, safe and sound.

And it was perfect.

# Chapter Four

## Kidnapped!

The next morning, we read our poems out loud. Nicole Rodriguez went first.

"There once was a goldfish named Goldie.
I loved her and I know she loved me.
The day that she died,
My mom threw her outside,
So the bowl wouldn't get gross and
moldy."

Next came Bigs Maloney.

"When springtime comes, I like to smell
All the flowers people sell.
Roses and carnations, too —
Red and yellow, pink and blue.
When I grow up I want to be
A wrestler or a florist, see?
I'll have my own big flower place,
And if you laugh, I'll smash your face."

I tried not to laugh. I tried really hard. When a guy as big as Bigs Maloney writes a love poem about flowers, the smartest thing you can do is keep quiet.

But sometimes it's hard to be smart.

Mike Radcliffe read his poem about dirt bikes. Danika Starling read a poem about her dad. I shifted around in my seat. I couldn't wait until it was my turn. And then, finally, it was.

My poem was a haiku. That meant it had to have seventeen syllables. Five syllables in the

first line and the last line, and seven syllables in the middle. It was short, just like me.

"Rags eats, sleeps, and drools.
Not the smartest dog ever,
But he's my best friend."

Then I showed the class the picture I drew of Rags chewing on a bone:

"That was lovely, Jigsaw," Ms. Gleason said. "You are all such wonderful poets, you deserve a special treat. Something I love very much." She walked over to the pink flowered sheet. She grabbed it. We all held our breath. "Surprise!" she exclaimed, whipping the sheet away.

There was dead silence.

On the corner of Ms. Gleason's desk sat a giant gumball machine. And inside the gumball machine? There was a whole lot of nothing much.

Surprise!

# Chapter Five
## Chocolate-Covered Clues

Ms. Gleason's face went from confused to mad to sad. It took about ten seconds. "On Monday, I filled this with Hershey's Kisses," she said sternly. "Where did they go?"

No one said anything. Most people looked down at their desks.

Athena raised her hand. "I have an idea," she said. "Jigsaw is a detective. Maybe *he* could figure out where the candy went."

Ms. Gleason nodded. And just like that, Mila and I had a new case. I pulled out my

detective notebook and my favorite red marker. I opened to a fresh page and wrote:

The Case of the Kidnapped Candy

At recess, Mila and I stayed inside the classroom and went on a hunt for clues. Being a detective sometimes means giving up recess.

Mila searched the room while I checked out the scene of the crime. There was nothing suspicious on Ms. Gleason's desk. Nothing on her chair. And then I saw a crumpled-up silver wrapper under the desk.

"I found something!" I called to Mila.

"I did, too!" she called back from the cubbies. So I grabbed the wrapper and hurried over to her. I held out my hand, palm side up. She did the same. We stared down at a matching pair of silver wrappers.

My eyes widened. "Where did you find yours?"

She pointed toward one of the cubbies. I looked up to see the name taped to the wall: Mike Radcliffe.

Our first suspect.

"I found something else, too," Mila said. She handed me a scrap of lined paper:

Meter: The rhythm of a poem

"So?" I asked. "It's part of our poetry vocabulary homework."

"Turn it over," Mila suggested.

I did. There was a brown smudge on the back. A familiar-looking smudge. I brought it to my nose and took a big whiff. Chocolate.

I pulled out my detective journal. Mila and I listed all the clues we had found. Then it was time to make our list of suspects.

Mike Radcliffe, I wrote.

"What about Bobby Solofsky?" Mila asked.

I nodded. Earlier that week I heard Solofsky bragging that he knew what was under the sheet. I ignored him like I always did. But now it made me wonder. Besides, Solofsky digs up trouble like Rags digs up bones.

"Anyone else?" I asked, hoping there wasn't. Our list was long enough.

"Joey," Mila said. "He was the Board Cleaner this week. That means he was in the classroom every day after school. And you know Joey . . ."

I sighed and wrote down his name. I *did* know Joey. He's a great guy. But he's also the kind of guy who would sell his mother for an Oreo cookie. Who knew what he would do for a gumball machine full of Hershey's Kisses?

"That's it," I said, closing the notebook. At the last minute, Mila stuck her finger between the pages.

"One more suspect," she insisted. She flipped the notebook open again. "Ms. Gleason."

*"What?"* I yelped. "Are you crazy? Why would she kidnap her own candy?"

"She did say she loved it more than anything," Mila pointed out. "Maybe she

didn't want to share. And you *did* find a wrapper under her desk."

I was sure Ms. Gleason was innocent. But I wrote her name down, anyway. There's one thing I've learned as a detective: Anything can happen.

And it usually does.

# Chapter Six

## Sweet and Sour

At lunch on Monday, Mila and I started investigating our suspects.

Mila was singing as we walked through the cafeteria. The tune sounded like that old nursery rhyme *"Frère Jacques."* But the words were a little . . . different.

*"Kidnapped candy, kidnapped candy,*
*Where are you? Where are you?*
*We would like to eat you. We would like to eat you,*
*Right away. Right away."*

"That's great," I told her. "It's just like a poem."

"Can a song be a poem?" she asked.

We both shrugged. It was a good question. But we had plenty of other questions to answer first. So we got down to business. Solofsky sat at the very end of a long table, stuffing french fries up his nose. Mike Radcliffe and Eddie Becker were cheering him on.

"We need to talk to you, Solofsky," I told him.

"Wait your turn, Jigsaw," Eddie complained. "I bet Bobby that he couldn't fit three fries up his nose."

Just then, Solofsky mashed one more fry into his nostril. "Pay up, Eddie!" he hooted. "I *never* lose."

Good thing I was done with lunch. Yeesh.

Eddie pulled a cupcake out of his lunch bag and slid it across the table. "This stinks," he grumbled. "Especially after our other bet —"

"Whaddaya want, *Theodore*?" Solofsky suddenly interrupted, turning to me. I could tell he didn't want me to hear what Eddie was about to say.

"We hear you found out about the candy surprise before the rest of us," Mila said.

Solofsky snorted. "Aw, you guys'll believe anything. That was just talk. I didn't know nothing."

"You didn't know *anything*," Mila corrected him.

"Exactly," Solofsky said, bobbing his head up and down. "Now you got the idea."

"And why should we believe you?" I asked.

Solofsky jerked his finger toward Mike. "Tell 'em," he ordered.

"Bobby didn't know anything," Mike said. He sounded like a robot.

"How about you?" I asked. "We found a Hershey's Kiss wrapper in front of your cubby. Know anything about that?"

Mike's face got red. "What were you doing snooping around my cubby?" he asked angrily. "Who said you could—"

"Mike doesn't eat chocolate," Solofsky interrupted. "He hates it. So it couldn't have been his wrapper."

"Uh, yeah, that's right," Mike agreed. "I hate chocolate. Blech."

Mila gave me a look that said: *Yeah, right.* I gave her a look back: *We're done here.* I was sure that somebody was lying — I just didn't know who.

We found Joey sitting at the other end of the table, next to Lucy Hiller and Bigs Maloney.

"I was never alone in the classroom, Jigsaw," Joey said, after he heard my question. He peeled the top off his peanut butter sandwich and dumped a bag of potato chips on top. Then he put the top slice of bread back on and took a giant bite. *"Mmmmph mmm mmmmph,"* he mumbled, crunching down on his mouthful of sticky chips. "Right, Lucy?"

Lucy wrinkled her nose. "That's *so* gross," she said, rolling her eyes at him.

"Uh, I don't think that's what he was asking you," Mila pointed out.

"Oh, right. Joey was never alone in the room," Lucy said quickly. "I was the Zookeeper last week. I fed the hamsters right after school, while Joey was cleaning the

erasers. We were there together every day last week. Neither of us peeked under the sheet."

*"Mmmph!"* Joey agreed. At least, I think he agreed.

I sighed. We still had three suspects, no leads, plenty of questions, and not a single piece of chocolate.

This whole case was starting to remind me of Shakespeare — I had a hard time figuring it out.

# Chapter Seven

## The Write Stuff

"Someone must be lying," I complained to Mila. "But who?"

"We still have one more suspect to add to our list," Mila reminded me.

"Who?"

She pulled out the slip of paper with the chocolate smudge on it. "Let's find out who this belongs to."

Mila showed me a book she got from the school library. It was called *Write and Wrong: A Handbook of Handwriting.* "It has lots of detective tips," Mila said. "It can help us

figure out who this handwriting belongs to. We just need samples of everyone else's handwriting."

"I know exactly where we can get them," I said.

A couple of hours later, Mila and I were sitting in the back of Room 201. Everyone else had gone home. But Ms. Gleason let us stay after school. She also let us use the class's poems for handwriting samples. We

had a huge stack of poems to go through. And it was going *verrrry* slowly.

Matching handwriting was tough. Here are some of the questions Mila's book told us to ask:

*Which direction do the letters slant?*
*What kind of pen was used?*
*How tall are the letters?*

We looked through lots of poems:

Donut Day, by Joey Pignattano
Mushy, squishy, tasty, sweet
Donuts that I love to eat.
Chocolate covered, filled with cream,
Donut day is like a dream.

My Favorite Hobby, by Bobby Solofsky
There once was this guy named Bobby.
He had a real favorite hobby.
He made people trip

And fall splat on their hip
And that's why everyone said the coolest guy in school was Bobby.

Wheeple Cushion! by Ralphie Jordan
When I stick you on my dad's chair,
or on my brother Justin's bed,
you make that funny phfeeftz-ing sound.
I laugh until my face turns red.

But there was no match. Nothing even came close. I was about to give up. And then my eyes widened. My mouth dropped open. And the little hairs on the back of my neck jumped to attention.

My best pink sweater
Has a hole in the collar
But I still love it.

I made Mila take a look.

Solofsky
Lucy Hiller
My best pink sweater
Has a hole in the collar
But I still love

"It's a haiku, just like yours," she said.

"You know what else it's just like?" I asked. "Look at the way the *a's* are written. And how thick the letters are."

"And the neat, even spacing," Mila added in an excited voice. "It looks just like . . ."

"Just like our mystery writer!" I said. I checked the name at the top of the page. Lucy Hiller.

I remembered that Lucy was Joey's alibi. She said that he was never in the classroom by himself. And now she was the one with chocolate on her hands.

Was it just a coincidence? Maybe.

But maybe not.

# Chapter Eight

## Live in Concert

We were standing in the back corner of Room 201, waiting for class to start. All I had to do was show Lucy the scrap paper with the chocolate smudge. And she knew I had proof.

"I did it," she admitted.

At last, the mystery was solved.

Or so I thought.

"Where did you stash the candy?" I asked.

Lucy's face got red. "Nowhere! There is no stash. I just took one piece."

"If you only took one piece, why did you lie about it?" I asked.

She looked down. "Because I knew what you'd think. But I swear, I didn't steal the candy. I didn't even *look* under the sheet! I just stuck my hand in and twisted the lever. The candy popped right out."

I didn't say anything. Part of me wanted to believe her. But the other part of me liked it better when I had solved the case.

Lucy nibbled her lip. It looked like

she wanted to say something else, but she didn't. We were both silent for a long time. "If you don't believe me, ask Joey," she said suddenly. "He was there, too. It was his idea."

Hmmm. So Joey had lied, too. I couldn't wait to find out why.

But before I could do that, it was time for schoolwork.

"This morning, we have a special treat," Ms. Gleason announced to the class. "Athena Lorenzo's father is here. He is going to give us a poetry concert."

None of us knew what that meant.

Mr. Lorenzo walked into the classroom. He was carrying a guitar. That seemed kind of weird. Then things got even weirder. He started to sing! He played three songs, and he was really good. But when he stopped, I was still confused.

I raised my hand. "Where's the poetry, Ms. Gleason?" Ms. Gleason and Mr. Lorenzo

both laughed. I waited for them to let me in on the joke.

"Songs *are* poetry," Ms. Gleason explained. "Poetry set to music. We call that kind of poetry *lyrics*."

Kim Lewis raised her hand. "But songs aren't *just* words. What about the music? Isn't that the important part?"

Mr. Lorenzo put down his guitar and walked over to the board. He wrote:

Lyrics
Melody

"You're right," he said. "Both of those matter a lot when you're making music. What else is important?"

We called out lots of words:

Rhythm
Rhyme

Voice

Instruments

Mr. Lorenzo wrote everything on the board. "They're *all* important," he said. "They all work together to make a good song."

"Just like the parts of a poem!" Ralphie exclaimed.

"Exactly," Ms. Gleason agreed. "Every piece works together to create the song."

"Like a jigsaw puzzle," I said.

Then Mr. Lorenzo had an idea. He asked Ms. Gleason for one of our poems. She gave him Athena's:

I always love
A rainy day,
A cloudy sky,
The world all gray.
Splishing, splashing

Puddles for play.
That's why I love
A rainy day.

He stared at it for a few minutes. He bounced his head back and forth, like he was listening to a beat the rest of us couldn't hear. Then he started pointing to people and giving us jobs.

Bigs Maloney had to tap slow, steady beats on his desk, like this: *bang, bang, bang.* Nicole Rodriguez had to clap her hands in a funny rhythm, like this: *claaaap, clap-clap, claaap, clap-clap*. Geetha Nair and Kim Lewis had to hum a long note, one high and one low. Together, they sounded like: *mmmmmmm*. Joey had to rub two erasers together: *scritch scritch scratch, scritch scritch*

*scratch.* Mila and I got a melody to sing, over and over: *dee dee dah deeee, dee dee dah deeee.* It was a lot of noise, and not much else.

Then Mr. Lorenzo started to play a slow, simple melody on his guitar. He pointed at Bigs and Nicole and they started to bang and clap. Then Geetha and Kim joined in with their humming and Joey rubbed his erasers. Mila and I started *dee-dee-dah-deeee*-ing. Mr. Lorenzo sang the words to Athena's poem in a clear, loud voice.

And suddenly we weren't a bunch of kids making noises anymore. We were an orchestra.

# Chapter Nine

## Irresistible

I cornered Joey on the playground. He was dribbling a big rubber ball. "Where's the candy?" I asked, before he could say anything. The ball dribbled away. Joey froze. He stared at me with his mouth wide open.

Nothing strange about that. Joey's mouth is always wide open. Of course, it's usually full of food.

I knew I'd found the candy thief. "Lucy told me everything," I said.

Joey shrugged. "Great! Then you know I just took one piece. Lucy and I agreed to keep it a secret. But I knew you'd believe us."

"Just one piece?" I repeated. I had a funny feeling in my stomach. And it wasn't because I'd swallowed a whoopie cushion. Joey was my friend — but I didn't believe him. That funny feeling was doubt. After all, someone had to have taken the candy. And all signs pointed to Joey.

Joey eats when he's nervous. He eats when he's happy. He eats when he's upset. And when he's tired. And when he's bored. And whenever you put food in front of him. This time, he had been alone in a room with a chocolate-filled gumball machine. Could he really have just walked away?

"Okay, so you just took one piece," I said. "How did you know it was there?"

"Oh, I didn't look under the sheet!" he said quickly. "Ms. Gleason told us not to, remember?"

I nodded. I remembered. It was starting to seem like I was the only one who did.

"I overheard Eddie telling a couple guys about it," Joey said.

"Eddie?" I repeated.

"Yeah," Joey said. He threw his arms out to his sides. "I just couldn't resist, Jigsaw! I stuck my hand under the sheet and turned the lever. One Kiss popped out. That's all I took. Honest!"

"Just one?" I asked.

"Well . . ." Joey rubbed the back of his neck. "Two. Okay . . . three. But that's it. Really."

But before I could ask anything else, Mila came up behind us. She slipped me a note. It was in code:

MIK ER ADCLI FF EIS EATI NG ACH OCOLA TE B AR!

Right away, I figured out that she was using a space code. I just had to push some of the letters together and move some of them farther apart. It only took me a couple minutes to solve the code: Mike Radcliffe is eating a chocolate bar!

"Is it true?" I asked Mila.

"Is what true?" Joey asked.

Mila just nodded and pointed toward the jungle gym. There was Mike, stuffing his face, hanging out with Eddie Becker and Bobby Solofsky.

MIKER ADCLI FF
EIS EATI NG ACH
OCOLA TE B AR!

I thought fast. Mike told me that he didn't like chocolate. Bobby backed him up. Here was proof that they were both lying. And I had been so sure that Joey was the real thief!

No wonder nothing added up about this case. It seemed like everyone in Room 201 had forgotten how to tell the truth.

"Let's go," I told Mila. "They've got some explaining to do."

# Chapter Ten

## Everybody Lies

As Mila and I walked up, Bobby Solofsky jumped off the jungle gym and put his fists on his hips. "No girls allowed," he said.

"Chill out, Solofsky," I said. "We just want to ask Eddie something."

Solofsky snorted. He ran his tongue over his front teeth with a loud, sucking sound. He rolled his eyes. Then he jabbed his finger toward me. "*You* can do whatever you want. But *she's* gotta go."

"Yeah," Mike yelled. "We're having an important meeting. No girls allowed!"

Mila shrugged. She started to walk away. But I grabbed her arm. Mila and I were partners. I wasn't going to let some silly rule split us up. Besides, Mila wasn't just some *girl*. She was . . . Mila.

"If that's what you want," I said, "we'll both go. We should probably tell Ms. Gleason what we just found out, anyway." I gave Mila a look. She got the idea.

"Yes, she'll want to know about Eddie and the chocolate," she added quickly.

"What about me and chocolate?" Eddie asked, his eyes darting toward us.

"Joey told us everything," I bragged. "We know *you* found out what was under the sheet. And you were probably the one who —"

"It was Bobby!" Eddie cried.

Solofsky whirled around. He glared at Eddie and growled. But Eddie didn't notice. He was too busy spilling the beans.

"Bobby was bragging that he knew what was under the sheet," Eddie said. "I bet him that he didn't. So he told me all about the gumball machine."

I stared at Solofsky. If looks could freeze, he'd be a Popsicle by now. I should have known it was him from the beginning.

"Don't look at me like that, *Theodore*," Solofsky said. "I'm not the thief."

"Yeah, right." I started to turn away. I know he was lying. Solofsky had to be the candynapper.

"Ask Eddie when he took his last piece of candy!" Bobby shouted.

I stopped. I asked. Eddie said it was Thursday afternoon, after school. The candy had turned up missing Friday morning.

"See?" Solofsky said in triumph. "I wasn't even there on Thursday afternoon. I went home early for a dentist's appointment. So I can't be the thief. There was still candy in the gumball machine after I left!"

Mila frowned. "He's right, Jigsaw. I remember he went home early."

I scowled. "Are you sure the candy was still there on Thursday?" I asked Eddie.

"I didn't see it," he said. "I just stuck my hand under the sheet and turned the lever. But a Hershey's Kiss popped right out. And it was definitely Thursday afternoon."

Mila and I both sighed. Just like that, our case was blown wide open. I started to walk away. But Mila stopped suddenly. "One more question," Mila said. "How did you find out about the candy?" she asked Solofsky.

Mike suddenly looked away. I remembered how he lied to us about not liking chocolate. And I was pretty sure I knew the answer to Mila's question.

"I found some Kisses in Mike's backpack last week," Solofsky admitted. "I made him tell me where they came from."

"Don't look at me like that, Jigsaw," Mike cried. "*I'm* not the thief. I only took a couple pieces. That's it." Mike climbed up to the top of the jungle gym. He scanned the playground. Then he pointed toward the basketball court. "I heard about the candy from Ralphie. Maybe *he's* the thief. Go ask him!"

Ralphie? It was starting to feel like everybody was a suspect. Ralphie admitted

that he knew about the candy, too. He said he took one piece on Wednesday morning, right before school.

He heard about it from Kim Lewis. Who heard about it from Helen Zuckerman. Who heard about it from Danika Starling. Who came to class early on Monday morning and saw *Ms. Gleason* sneaking a piece of chocolate. Huh?

We were a little closer to the truth.

But we were still miles away from an answer.

# Chapter Eleven

## Too Many Questions

I slumped down at the kitchen table. I glanced at the long list of suspects in my detective notebook. At this point, the only people who weren't suspects were the Easter Bunny and the Tooth Fairy.

Yeesh. I had written down the name of almost everyone in Room 201. But I still didn't know who the one true thief was. I didn't know anything for sure. None of the clues pointed to a definite candynapper. After all, it seemed like I had caught everyone lying at least once. Maybe they were still lying. Maybe Bobby, Mike, and Eddie were messing with me. Or maybe Joey took the candy and Lucy was covering for him. Or maybe Mila was right all along, and Ms. Gleason kept it for herself. Or maybe . . .

I had to lay my head down on the table and close my eyes. This case was giving me a giant headache.

You know what else was giving me a headache? My brothers. Nick and Daniel were *supposed* to be washing the dishes.

And they were. Sort of. Mostly they were splashing soap bubbles at each other. And yelling. Really loudly.

They were arguing about basketball. In the winter, that's almost all they ever do. Sure, sometimes they watch basketball. Sometimes they play it. But mostly, they argue about it.

"The point guard is the most important position!" Nick claimed. He banged a pot in the sink.

"No, it's the center," Daniel argued. "Every team needs a big guy to get rebounds and block shots."

"The point guard dribbles the ball," Nick countered. "He makes passes and shoots from the outside."

*"Mmmmmmmph,"* I groaned. "*Urgggggggggg.* Stop arguing. Please." I pressed my hands over my ears.

That's when my brothers noticed I was in the room.

"What do you think, Worm?" Nick asked. "Come on, tell him the point guard is the MVP."

"More like MVPETC," Daniel snapped. "Most Valuable Player Except The Center! Tell him, Shorty."

"Don't call me Shorty," I complained. "Or Worm." Then I stopped talking and started thinking. Anything was better than worrying about the candy case.

Nick was right, the point guard was important. He ran the offense. But so was the center, just like Daniel said. The team needed tall players. So who was the most valuable player?

I suddenly remembered what Ms. Gleason said about all the parts of the poem working together.

I remembered Mr. Lorenzo giving everyone little jobs and turning our class into an orchestra.

And just like that, I knew who had kidnapped the candy.

I raced out of the room to call Mila.

"Where are you going?" Nick called after me.

"You didn't say who was right!" Daniel yelled.

"You both are!" I called back. But I didn't stop to explain.

I had a case to close.

# Chapter Twelve
## The Blame Game

First thing in the morning, I asked Ms. Gleason if I could say something to the class.

"Did you solve the case, Jigsaw?" she asked.

I shook my head. "Not yet. But I'm about to."

Mila stood next to me. I was a little nervous. Then Mila winked at me, which helped. I was ready.

"So, who dunnit?" Eddie Becker called out.

"Theodore did!" Solofsky shouted. "Now he's going to confess."

"Let Jigsaw talk," Ms. Gleason said in a stern voice. "I think we all want to hear what he has to say."

"This case took me a long time to solve," I told them. "It was tougher than month-old caramels. There were lots of suspects. Joey and Lucy were in the classroom alone. They could have —"

"We didn't do it!" they cried together.

"And then there was Mike and Bobby, who —"

"You can't pin this on me, *Theodore*!" Bobby said angrily.

"Like I said, I had a lot of suspects," I went on in a louder voice. "But none of them seemed quite right. Then I figured it out."

They all stared at me, eyes wide.

"Everybody close your eyes," I said.

The whole class kept staring right at me.

"Let's close our eyes now, class," Ms. Gleason said.

I gave her a grateful smile. “Uh, you, too, Ms. Gleason,” I said nervously. “Please?”

The class giggled. Ms. Gleason looked confused, but she closed her eyes. I took a deep breath.

“Now that everyone’s eyes are closed, raise your hand if you snuck a piece of candy this week.” No one moved. I glanced at Mila, alarmed. What if this didn’t work? What if I was wrong?

Then, very slowly, Danika Starling raised her hand. A moment later, Kim Lewis raised hers. Then Lucy Hiller. Eddie Becker. Joey Pignattano. And more, and more. Until finally, almost every kid in the class had their hand up in the air. Even Ms. Gleason’s hand crept toward the ceiling. I knew it!

“Open your eyes!” I called out. Everyone’s eyes shot open before their hands had time to come down.

There was a moment of silence. The class was craning their necks around, looking to see whose hand was up.

"Not just one person kidnapped the candy, Ms. Gleason," I explained. "That was my mistake. I had started out looking for one thief, when I should have been looking for many thieves. Everyone played a part in this crime. Everyone is a little bit guilty."

"Even me," Ms. Gleason sheepishly admitted.

Ms. Gleason was happy that we didn't have a thief in Room 201. She said we had all learned our lesson.

And as for me? I was happy, too. Because the next morning, Ms. Gleason called me and Mila up to her desk. "Thank you for solving the case," she said. "I thought you deserved a reward. Especially since you two never got any Hershey's Kisses!" She handed us a giant box. Inside were four huge chocolate letters: LOVE.

It could take us a month to eat all that chocolate! So we decided to get started right away. Mila sliced off a little piece of the "V." I nibbled on the edge of the "L."

I still say love stinks.

But it sure tastes good.

## About the Author

James Preller often draws upon his own life as a basis for his Jigsaw Jones books. Like Jigsaw, James Preller has a slobbering, sock-eating dog. Like Jigsaw, James was the youngest in a large family. His older brothers called him Worm and worse — yeesh! And so do Jigsaw's!

James and Jigsaw both love jigsaw puzzles, baseball, grape juice, and mysteries! But even though Jigsaw and James have so much in common, they are not the same person.

Unlike Jigsaw, James Preller is the author of many books for children. He lives in Delmar, New York, with his wife, Lisa, three kids — Nicholas, Gavin, and Maggie — his two cats, and his dog.

**Learn more at www.jamespreller.com**

# If Your Dog Could Talk, What Would He Tell You?

New teacher Mr. Taylor can make up a great story using any five things his students choose. Give him a dog, a boat, a tennis ball, a playing card, and a necklace, and Mr. Taylor tells an exciting tale of a young girl who teaches her dog to talk and of the adventures they share.

SCHOLASTIC

LITTLE APPLE

SCHOLASTIC and associated logos are trademarks and/or registered trademarks of Scholastic Inc.